First published by Parragon in 2009

Parragon
Queen Street House
4 Queen Street
Bath BA1 1HE, UK

Copyright © Parragon Books Ltd 2009

ISBN 978-1-4075-8883-4

Printed in China

Bedtime Tales

PaRragon

Bath · New York · Singapore · Hong Kong · Cologne · Delhi · Melbourne

Princess Sleepyhead

Goodnight, Princess Sleepyhead!
It's time to climb the stairs to bed.
Tidy up. There's lots of mess!
Neatly hang your pretty dress.

Brush your teeth. Make sure they're clean.
Brush up and down until they gleam!
Put your jewels in their box.
Brush your long and silky locks.

Snuggle down, switch on your light.
It shines just like the stars at night.
Sleep tight beneath its cosy beams –
Goodnight, Princess. Have sweet dreams!

Mr Moon

Look through the window
At the moon shining bright.
Who can you see
In the twinkling starlight?

Up in the trees,
The grey doves coo.
Calling a friendly
"Good night" to you.

Good night, little squirrel.
Good night, little mouse.
Hurrying, scurrying to bed
In the house.

Listen to Owl calling,
"Who-whoo-whooo!"
While old Mr Moon
Watches over you.

Hamster Sleepover

Ali looked out of her bedroom window. There, at last, were her best friends coming up the garden path.

Ashley and Martha had sleeping bags under their arms. Daisy was holding a green duvet. They all saw her and waved.

"This is going to be the best sleepover party ever!" Ali said. She jumped off her bed and ran down the stairs two at a time.

After a supper of pizza and chocolate cake – everyone's favourite – the girls got ready for bed.

"Ali has never wanted to go to bed this early before!" joked her mum.

As the four friends snuggled down for the night in Ali's room, there was a loud scratching noise at the bedroom door.

"What's that?" asked Daisy.

They all heard a loud miaow.

"It's Tiger!" said Ali with a grin. Tiger was Ali's cat. "I think she wants to come in and play!"

"Should I let her in?" asked Martha, getting up.

There was a sudden shout from Daisy. "No! Don't open the door!" she said. "Where's Lulu? She isn't in her cage!"

The girls all looked at the hamster cage in the corner of the room. Daisy was right. Ali's hamster, Lulu, was missing.

"Oh no!" said Ali. "We have to find her! Quick!"

The girls began a mad hunt for Lulu, while Tiger scratched at the bedroom door.

"Hang on, Tiger!" Ashley called. "You can't come in yet!"

Daisy searched under Ali's bed. Ashley looked through the pile of sleeping bags. Martha checked behind the bookcase. There was no sign of Lulu.

Ali opened a drawer. "Sometimes she likes to sleep in my socks," she said. But Lulu wasn't there either.

"Where can she be?" Ali groaned.

Just then, Martha spotted something. "Look!" she said.

The girls laughed. They had found Lulu at last, curled up fast asleep in one of Ali's pink slippers.

"She's having her very own sleepover!" Ali said.

The Lost Boots

Zack really wanted to get into the Space School powerball team. He had begged Mum to buy him some brand-new jet boots, and he practised all weekend before the trials.

But on the morning of the trials, Zack's new boots were not in his locker.

The old pair he borrowed were too big for him. During the trial's warm-up Zack tripped up and landed on his back. He knew he would never make the team.

Zack limped off the court sadly, but Coach Cooper turned and stopped him.

"I know how much you want to be in this team, Zack," he said. "So I'm going to make you a reserve. Don't worry, your time will come."

At the match Zack sat on the bench, watching his team warm up.

"See how a real player does it," said Baz, the team captain. He fired a powerball straight at Zack.

"Baz, I saw that," said Coach Cooper. "You're off my team."

"It's a stupid game, anyway!" shouted Baz. He stormed out,

kicking off his jet boots.

Zack looked at the jet boots. They were just like the lost boots… In fact, they *were* his boots. Baz must have stolen them!

"Your turn, Zack!" said Coach Cooper. Zack couldn't believe his luck. He was in the powerball team.

The match began. Both teams were scoring well. Every player wanted to win. With a minute to go, Zack's team were trailing by a point. Zack switched his boots to turbo charge, and leaped into the air. He slammed the ball at the scoring plate, and it dropped neatly through the target.

The buzzer blew. Zack's school team were the champions. Zack had won the match!

"Well done, Zack," said Coach Cooper. "We've never won the trophy before!" Everyone cheered.

Pyjama Party Disco

It was the school holidays. Ali, Martha and Ashley were at Daisy's for a sleepover.

"Let's have a disco!" said Daisy as they munched on some crisps. "We can use my new disco ball lamp."

"Great idea!" said the others.

Daisy got out her best music for dancing to, and the others looked through Daisy's wardrobe for party clothes to wear.

Once they had all changed, the girls cleared a space on Daisy's bedroom floor and closed the curtains. Daisy put on the music and Ashley switched on the disco ball lamp.

The girls started to sing and dance. Daisy picked up her hairbrush and jumped onto her bed. "Look at me!" she laughed. "I could be a popstar!" Her friends cheered as she sang along, pretending the hairbrush was a microphone.

Before long, Ashley, Ali and Martha were singing and dancing on the bed too.

Just as Ali was in the middle of a high kick there was a loud cracking noise and Daisy's bed collapsed.

Martha and Ashley landed on the floor in a heap, and Ali tripped forwards and crashed into Daisy.

Daisy's big brother Jon came rushing into the room. "What's going on in here?" he grinned. "Disco dancing accident?"

"It's not funny!" said Daisy. "We've broken the bed!"

"I could mend it," said Jon. "I might not even tell Mum. What's it worth?"

The girls looked at each other. "How about half a bar of chocolate?" said Martha.

Jon laughed. "No way! You'll have to do better than that!"

In the end the girls had to promise Jon *all* their sweets and crisps before he went to get the toolbox.

When Jon had fixed the bed the girls got into their pyjamas.

"The next time I'm disco dancing, it's going to be on a proper dance floor!" groaned Daisy.

"Or on stage in front of a huge audience!" laughed Ashley.

I Just Can't Sleep

It's time to sleep.
I've brushed my teeth
And read my book,
I've put my bathrobe
On the hook, and...
I just can't sleep.
The bed's too hot,
The light's too bright,
There are far too many
Sounds tonight, and...
Maybe I'll sleep.
I think I might,
I think I'll – yawn –
Turn out the light.
Good night.
Zzzzzz...

Bed in Summer

In winter I get up at night
And dress by yellow candle-light.
In summer quite the other way,
I have to go to bed by day.

I have to go to bed and see
The birds still hopping on the tree,
Or hear the grown-up people's feet
Still going past me in the street.

And does it not seem hard to you,
When all the sky is clear and blue,
And I should like so much to play,
To have to go to bed by day?

One Stormy Night

It was Patch's first night outside in his smart new kennel. He snuggled down on his blanket and watched as dusk fell.

Before long he fell fast asleep. As he slept, big spots of rain began to fall. A splash of water dripped from the kennel roof onto his nose.

Then there was a great crash and a bright flash of light lit up the sky.

Patch woke with a start and was on his feet at once, growling and snarling. "Just a silly storm," he told himself. "Nothing to scare a farm dog!"

But as the lightning flashed yet again, he saw a great shadow looming against the barn. Patch gulped. Whatever could it be? He began to bark furiously, trying to act braver than he felt – and sure enough, next time the lightning flashed, there was no sign of the shadow. "I soon scared that monster away!" he thought.

But as Patch settled back down, the sky outside lit up once more. There in the doorway towered the monster!

"Just checking you're okay in the storm," said Mummy.

"A fearless farm dog like me?" said Patch. "Of course I am!" But as the storm raged on, he snuggled up close to her all the same!

Now the Day Is Over

Now the day is over,
Night is drawing nigh,
Shadows of evening
Steal across the sky.

Now the darkness gathers,
Stars begin to peep,
Birds and beasts and flowers
Soon will be asleep.

The Elves and the Shoemaker

Once upon a time there was a kind old shoemaker. He worked hard, but the day came when he had only a few pennies left – just enough to buy leather for one final pair of shoes.

That evening the shoemaker cut up the leather. Then, leaving it on his workbench, he climbed the stairs to bed.

The next morning the shoemaker couldn't believe his eyes. On his workbench was the finest pair of shoes he had ever seen. He put the shoes in his shop window and that afternoon a fine gentleman bought them for a price that amazed the shoemaker.

The money was enough to buy enough leather to make two new pairs of shoes. The shoemaker cut up the leather and left it lying on his workbench. "I'll finish the shoes tomorrow," he yawned, and went to bed.

The next morning, when he came downstairs, the shoemaker saw two fine pairs of beautiful new shoes!

So it went on for weeks. Every night the shoemaker cut out the leather and left it on his workbench, and every morning there were splendid shoes waiting to be sold.

One night the shoemaker and his wife decided that they had to solve the mystery. So, after the shoemaker left the leather on his workbench, they shut up shop and hid in a cupboard.

When the clock struck midnight, two tiny elves appeared. They ran over to the workbench and began to stitch and sew, until they had made five pairs of shoes. Then they shot up the chimney.

"The elves must be frozen in those thin, tattered clothes," said the shoemaker. "And their feet are bare, although they make such beautiful shoes!"

So the shoemaker's wife made two little jackets and two pairs of trousers. The shoemaker made two pairs of tiny boots, fastened with shiny silver buckles. The next evening, they wrapped the little clothes in tissue paper and left them on the workbench. Then they hid in the cupboard and waited.

At the stroke of midnight, the elves appeared. When they opened the presents, they were overjoyed. They put on their new clothes and danced happily all around the shop, singing,

"See what handsome boys we are!
We will work on shoes no more!"

Then they flew up the chimney and were gone, never to return again! But the shoemaker and his wife never forgot them.

The Dragon's Cave

One fine sunny day, Sir Sam the Small was riding past a little village. He was just thinking about what to have for tea when the whole village came running out to meet him.

"A knight!" they shouted. "A knight!"

"That's right!" said Sir Sam, jumping down from his horse. "How can I help you?"

"There's a dragon living on top of the hill," a lady said. "We're afraid of him! His cave smokes night and day and we're scared that soon he'll get hungry and come down and eat us!"

"You're a knight. Can you save us from the dragon?" added a man.

"I'll certainly try," said Sir Sam.

Sir Sam went to the dragon's cave on top of the hill. The people were right. There were clouds of smoke coming from the cave. He took out his sword.

"Come out, dragon!" Sam called. "Come out and fight!"

The dragon came out. Now, Sir Sam had fought a lot of dragons. Big dragons. Fierce dragons. Dragons who would gobble up a village for breakfast, and then follow up with a town for lunch. This dragon didn't look very big or very scary.

"I just burned my toast," said the dragon to Sir Sam, grumpily. "Bother. I'm always doing that."

"The people in the village below are afraid of you, you know," said Sir Sam.

The dragon looked astonished. "Are they?" he asked. "Why on earth are they afraid of me?"

"It's the clouds of smoke," said Sir Sam. "I know, why don't you invite them to tea this afternoon? Then you can make friends."

"Great idea!" said the dragon.

Sir Sam went down to the village and told the people about the dragon. "He just wants to be friends," he said. "And he's invited you all to tea this afternoon."

Everyone went up to the dragon's cave. The dragon was delighted to see them. "Have some toast!" he said.

Sir Sam looked at the toast. It was very, very black.

"I think I'll stick to cakes, thanks," he said.

Sleepover Splash

In Ashley's bedroom Martha, Daisy and Ali were rolling out their sleeping bags for another sleepover.

"Max is driving me mad!" said Ashley. "I hate having a twin brother!"

All day long Max had been playing jokes on Ashley. He and his friend James had put a frog in her bed and spread mustard in her peanut-butter sandwiches. They had also hidden her ballet shoes so she was late for her lesson.

"Why don't you get your own back?" said Martha. She sat down on Ashley's bed. "Let's come up with a really good joke to play on him!"

"I know!" said Daisy. "Here's a good joke! Let's put a bucket

of water above his door. When he opens it he'll get soaked!"

"That's a great idea!" said Ashley, jumping up. "I'll go and get a bucket from downstairs and you all make sure Max is out of his room!"

Martha and Ali went out onto the

landing and knocked on Max's door. There was no answer. "All clear!" they called. Ashley came back up with the bucket, and she and Daisy took it to the bathroom to fill it with water.

Daisy climbed onto a chair and lifted up the bucket.

Ashley opened Max's door just enough so the bucket would balance on top. "Max!" she called. "There's something in your room for you!"

Ashley, Ali and Martha raced across the landing, back to Ashley's bedroom. "Quick, Daisy!" hissed Ashley.

But just as Max came up the stairs, Daisy lost her balance on the chair and, with a loud cry, tumbled down onto Max. The bucket toppled over, soaking them both from head to toe in icy-cold water!

Tent Trouble

Ross and Jane were on the swings in the campsite playground.

"This is great!" said Ross, pushing off as hard as he could.

Sam and Kim, who were staying in the tent next door to Ross and Jane, were watching Ross and Jane play.

"Swings are for babies," said Sam.

"It's fun," said Jane.

"We're going to have better fun," said Sam.

"What are you going to do?" asked Ross.

"We're not telling you," said Kim. And they ran off.

"I wonder what they're going to do?" said Jane.

"Let's follow them," said Ross.

Ross and Jane followed Sam and Kim across the campsite back to where their tents were pitched.

From behind the bushes, they watched Sam and Kim pulling out all the tent pegs in their parents' tent one by one

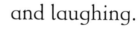

and laughing.

"Now this is fun!" Sam was saying to Kim.

"The tent is going to fall down!" said Jane to Ross.

"Look out!" shouted Ross, as loudly as he could.

Sam's mum and dad

looked out of the tent...
just as it fell down around
their ears with a huge
flapping noise!

"Ouch!" cried Sam and
Kim's dad, as a pole hit
him on the head.

Sam and Kim's parents
crawled out of the ruined
tent.

"I wonder what
happened?" said Sam and
Kim's dad. "We must have not put it up properly."

Sam and Kim were trying hard not to giggle.

Ross stepped out from behind the bushes.

"It wasn't the wind," he said. "Sam and Kim pulled out all
the tent pegs."

"They did," agreed Jane.

"Sam! Kim!" shouted
their parents.

"It was a joke!" said Sam.

"I have a better joke,"
said their mum. She picked
up the tent pegs and gave
them to Sam and Kim.

"Put the tent back up!"
she said.

Poor Peep

Sophie and Sam were playing in the garden when Miss Tring from next door came out of her house. "Peep!" she called. "Peep! Where are you?"

Peep was Miss Tring's cat.

"Is Peep missing, Miss Tring?" asked Sophie.

"Yes," said Miss Tring. "She's been missing since last night. I can't find her."

"We'll help you look for her," said Sam.

Sam and Sophie began to look. They looked all over their garden. Then Sophie heard a noise.

"What's that noise?" she said. "Where's it coming from?"

"Listen!" said Sam. The noise was coming from a big metal bin Sophie and Sam's dad sometimes used to keep garden rubbish in.

"Miaow! Miaow!" Sam ran to the bin and opened the lid. Peep was inside. She miaowed even louder.

They lifted Peep out and took her home to Miss Tring.

"She must have climbed in yesterday when Dad was working in the garden," said

Sophie to Miss Tring.

"I'm just glad she's home again," said Miss Tring.

"Miaow!" miaowed Peep, lifting up one of her front paws.

"Poor Peep! She has cut her paw!" said Sophie.

"We'll need to take her to the vet," said Miss Tring. "Would you like to come with me?"

"Yes, please!" said Sophie and Sam.

The vet stroked Peep. "Nothing serious, Peep," she said. "You'll soon be better." She cleaned Peep's paw and put a bandage on it.

"All better now, Peep!" said Sam, stroking her gently.

Peep began to purr.

Miss Tring smiled. "Thank you for helping!" she said.

Treasure Map

Pirate captain Jenny and her band of ruthless pirates were very excited. They were on the hunt for treasure!

Captain Jenny showed them all the treasure map. There was an 'X' marked on it. It was six steps from a rock.

"There'll be gold doubloons and silver sovereigns, rubies red as blood, sapphires bluer than the sky and diamonds worth more than this entire ship!" she said.

Billy the cabin boy was as excited as everyone else. "I'd really like a gold doubloon," he thought. "Just one." But he didn't think that he'd be allowed any of the treasure. He was too young.

The pirates landed on the beach. "Come on, me hearties!" cried Jenny, jumping off the ship into the shallows with a big splash.

On the beach there was a big rock, just as the treasure map had promised.

Captain Jenny took six steps to the left. "One, two, three, four, five, six."

"Here we go!" she cried.

"Hooray!" cheered the pirates. They started to dig a hole with their shovels in the hot sun. Soon everyone was sweating. They dug and dug and dug – but there was no treasure.

"Oh dear," said Captain Jenny.

"No treasure!" said Bosun Bob.

"Maybe it's a fake map," said Crewman Charlie.

They were all fed up. Then Billy looked at the map again.

"Er, Captain," he said.

"What, Billy?" said Captain Jenny.

"I think the map might be upside down," said Billy.

Captain Jenny looked at the map again. "Do you know, Billy, I think you might be right!" she said.

Captain Jenny took six steps to the right. "One, two, three, four, five, six."

The pirates dug a new hole.

"Treasure!" they all cried.

"Thanks to Billy," said Captain Jenny. "And as a reward, Billy, you can have a dozen gold doubloons!"